Hugh Selwyn

Hugh Selwyn Mauberley

by Ezra Pound

Copyright © 6/1/2015
Jefferson Publication

ISBN-13: 978-1514180853

Printed in the United States of America

All rights reserved. No part of this book may be reprinted or reproduced or utilized in any form or by any electronic, mechanical, or other means, now known or hereafter invented, including photocopying and recording, or in any form of storage or retrieval system, without prior permission in writing from the publisher.'

Contents

E.P. ODE POUR SELECTION DE SON SEPULCHRE 3
   I. 3
   II. 5
   III. 5
   IV. 7
   V. 8
YEUX GLAUQUES 8
"SIENA MI FE', DISFECEMI MAREMMA" 9
BRENNBAUM. 11
MR. NIXON 11
   X. 13
   XI. 13
   XII. 14
ENVOI (1919) 15
(MAUBERLEY) 17
   I. 17
   II. 17
"THE AGE DEMANDED" 20
VIDE POEM II. 20
   IV. 23
MEDALLION 24

E.P. ODE POUR SELECTION DE SON SEPULCHRE

I.

FOR three years, out of key with his time,
He strove to resuscitate the dead art

Of poetry; to maintain "the sublime"
In the old sense. Wrong from the start—

No hardly, but, seeing he had been born
In a half savage country, out of date;
Bent resolutely on wringing lilies from the acorn;
Capaneus; trout for factitious bait;

ἴδμεν γάρ τοι πάν πάνθ', ὅσ' ἐνὶ Τροίῃ
Caught in the unstopped ear;
Giving the rocks small lee-way
The chopped seas held him, therefore, that year.

His true Penelope was Flaubert,
He fished by obstinate isles;
Observed the elegance of Circe's hair
Rather than the mottoes on sun-dials.

Unaffected by "the march of events,"
He passed from men's memory in *l'an trentiesme*
De son eage; the case presents
No adjunct to the Muses' diadem.

II.

THE age demanded an image
Of its accelerated grimace,
Something for the modern stage,
Not, at any rate, an Attic grace;

Not, not certainly, the obscure reveries
Of the inward gaze;
Better mendacities
Than the classics in paraphrase!

The "age demanded" chiefly a mould in plaster,
Made with no loss of time,
A prose kinema, not, not assuredly, alabaster
Or the "sculpture" of rhyme.

III.

THE tea-rose tea-gown, etc.
Supplants the mousseline of Cos,
The pianola "replaces"
Sappho's barbitos.

Christ follows Dionysus,
Phallic and ambrosial

Made way for macerations;
Caliban casts out Ariel.

All things are a flowing,
Sage Heracleitus says;
But a tawdry cheapness
Shall reign throughout our days.

Even the Christian beauty
Defects—after Samothrace;
We see το καλόν
Decreed in the market place.

Faun's flesh is not to us,
Nor the saint's vision.
We have the press for wafer;
Franchise for circumcision.

All men, in law, are equals.
Free of Peisistratus,
We choose a knave or an eunuch
To rule over us.

O bright Apollo,
τίν' άνδρα, τίν' ήρωα, τίνα θεον,
What god, man, or hero
Shall I place a tin wreath upon!

IV.

THESE fought, in any case, and some
believing, pro domo, in any case .. Some
quick to arm, some for adventure, some
from fear of weakness, some from fear of
censure, some for love of slaughter, in
imagination, learning later . . .

some in fear, learning love of slaughter;
Died some "pro patria, non dulce non et decor"..

walked eye-deep in hell believing in old
men's lies, then unbelieving came home,
home to a lie, home to many deceits, home
to old lies and new infamy;

usury age-old and age-thick and liars in
public places.

Daring as never before, wastage as never before.
Young blood and high blood,
Fair cheeks, and fine bodies;

fortitude as never before

frankness as never before, disillusions as never told in the old days, hysterias, trench confessions, laughter out of dead bellies.

V.

THERE died a myriad,
And of the best, among them,
For an old bitch gone in the teeth,
For a botched civilization,

Charm, smiling at the good mouth,
Quick eyes gone under earth's lid,

For two gross of broken statues,
For a few thousand battered books.

YEUX GLAUQUES

GLADSTONE was still respected,
When John Ruskin produced
"Kings Treasuries"; Swinburne
And Rossetti still abused.

Fœtid Buchanan lifted up his voice
When that faun's head of hers
Became a pastime for
Painters and adulterers.

The Burne-Jones cartons
Have preserved her eyes;
Still, at the Tate, they teach
Cophetua to rhapsodize;

Thin like brook-water,
With a vacant gaze.
The English Rubaiyat was still-born
In those days.

The thin, clear gaze, the same
Still darts out faun-like from the half-ruin'd
fac
Questing and passive ....
"Ah, poor Jenny's case"...

Bewildered that a world
Shows no surprise
At her last maquero's
Adulteries.

"SIENA MI FE', DISFECEMI MAREMMA"

AMONG the pickled foetuses and bottled bones,
Engaged in perfecting the catalogue,
I found the last scion of the

Senatorial families of Strasbourg, Monsieur
Verog.

For two hours he talked of Gallifet;
Of Dowson; of the Rhymers' Club;
Told me how Johnson (Lionel) died
By falling from a high stool in a pub . . .

But showed no trace of alcohol
At the autopsy, privately performed—
Tissue preserved—the pure mind
Arose toward Newman as the whiskey
warmed.

Dowson found harlots cheaper than hotels;
Headlam for uplift; Image impartially
imbued
With raptures for Bacchus, Terpsichore and
the Church.
So spoke the author of "The Dorian Mood",

M. Verog, out of step with the decade,
Detached from his contemporaries,
Neglected by the young,
Because of these reveries.

BRENNBAUM.

THE sky-like limpid eyes,
The circular infant's face,
The stiffness from spats to collar
Never relaxing into grace;

The heavy memories of Horeb, Sinai and the forty years,
Showed only when the daylight fell
Level across the face
Of Brennbaum "The Impeccable".

MR. NIXON

IN the cream gilded cabin of his steam yacht
Mr. Nixon advised me kindly, to advance with fewer
Dangers of delay. "Consider
   "Carefully the reviewer.

"I was as poor as you are;
"When I began I got, of course,
"Advance on royalties, fifty at first", said Mr. Nixon,
"Follow me, and take a column,
"Even if you have to work free.

"Butter reviewers. From fifty to three hundred
"I rose in eighteen months;
"The hardest nut I had to crack
"Was Dr. Dundas.

"I never mentioned a man but with the view
"Of selling my own works.
"The tip's a good one, as for literature
"It gives no man a sinecure."

And no one knows, at sight a masterpiece.
And give up verse, my boy,
There's nothing in it.

* * *

Likewise a friend of Bloughram's once advised me:
Don't kick against the pricks,
Accept opinion. The "Nineties" tried your game
And died, there's nothing in it.

X.

BENEATH the sagging roof
The stylist has taken shelter,
Unpaid, uncelebrated,
At last from the world's welter

Nature receives him,
With a placid and uneducated mistress
He exercises his talents
And the soil meets his distress.

The haven from sophistications and contentions
Leaks through its thatch;
He offers succulent cooking;
The door has a creaking latch.

XI.

"CONSERVATRIX of Milésien"
Habits of mind and feeling,
Possibly. But in Ealing
With the most bank-clerkly of Englishmen?

No, "Milésien" is an exaggeration.
No instinct has survived in her

Older than those her grandmother
Told her would fit her station.

XII.

"DAPHNE with her thighs in bark
Stretches toward me her leafy hands",—
Subjectively. In the stuffed-satin drawing-
room
I await The Lady Valentine's commands,

Knowing my coat has never been
Of precisely the fashion
To stimulate, in her,
A durable passion;

Doubtful, somewhat, of the value
Of well-gowned approbation
Of literary effort,
But never of The Lady Valentine's vocation:

Poetry, her border of ideas,
The edge, uncertain, but a means of
blending
With other strata
Where the lower and higher have ending;

A hook to catch the Lady Jane's attention,
A modulation toward the theatre,
Also, in the case of revolution,
A possible friend and comforter.

* * *

Conduct, on the other hand, the soul
"Which the highest cultures have nourished"
To Fleet St. where
Dr. Johnson flourished;

Beside this thoroughfare
The sale of half-hose has
Long since superseded the cultivation
Of Pierian roses.

ENVOI (1919)

GO, dumb-born book,
Tell her that sang me once that song of
Lawes;
Hadst thou but song
As thou hast subjects known,
Then were there cause in thee that should
condone

Even my faults that heavy upon me lie
And build her glories their longevity.

Tell her that sheds
Such treasure in the air,
Recking naught else but that her graces give
Life to the moment,
I would bid them live
As roses might, in magic amber laid,
Red overwrought with orange and all made
One substance and one colour
Braving time.

Tell her that goes
With song upon her lips
But sings not out the song, nor knows
The maker of it, some other mouth,
May be as fair as hers,
Might, in new ages, gain her worshippers,
When our two dusts with Waller's shall be laid,
Siftings on siftings in oblivion,
Till change hath broken down
All things save Beauty alone.

1920

(MAUBERLEY)

I.

TURNED from the "eau-forte
Par Jaquemart"
To the strait head
Of Mcssalina:

"His true Penelope
Was Flaubert",
And his tool
The engraver's

Firmness,
Not the full smile,
His art, but an art
In profile;

Colourless
Pier Francesca,
Pisanello lacking the skill
To forge Achaia.

II.

*"Qu'est ce qu'ils savent de
l'amour, et gu'est ce qu'ils peuvent*

> *comprendre? S'ils ne comprennent pas la poèsie, s'ils ne sentent pas la musique, qu'est ce qu'ils peuvent comprendre de cette passion en comparaison avec laquelle la rose est grossière et le parfum des violettes un tonnerre?"* CAID ALI

FOR three years, diabolus in the scale,
He drank ambrosia,
All passes, ANANGKE prevails,
Came end, at last, to that Arcadia.

He had moved amid her phantasmagoria,
Amid her galaxies,
NUKTIS AGALMA

Drifted….drifted precipitate,
Asking time to be rid of….
Of his bewilderment; to designate
His new found orchid….

To be certain….certain…
(Amid aerial flowers)..time for arrangements—

Drifted on
To the final estrangement;

Unable in the supervening blankness
To sift TO AGATHON from the chaff
Until he found his seive…
Ultimately, his seismograph:

—Given, that is, his urge
To convey the relation
Of eye-lid and cheek-bone
By verbal manifestation;

To present the series
Of curious heads in medallion—

He had passed, inconscient, full gaze,
The wide-banded irises
And botticellian sprays implied
In their diastasis;

Which anæsthesis, noted a year late,
And weighed, revealed his great affect,
(Orchid), mandate
Of Eros, a retrospect.

. . .

Mouths biting empty air,
The still stone dogs,
Caught in metamorphosis were,
Left him as epilogues.

"THE AGE DEMANDED"

VIDE POEM II.

FOR this agility chance found
Him of all men, unfit
As the red-beaked steeds of
The Cytheræan for a chain-bit.

The glow of porcelain
Brought no reforming sense
To his perception
Of the social inconsequence.

Thus, if her colour
Came against his gaze,
Tempered as if
It were through a perfect glaze

He made no immediate application
Of this to relation of the state
To the individual, the month was more
temperate

Because this beauty had been
> ......
>> The coral isle, the lion-coloured sand
>> Burst in upon the porcelain revery:
>> Impetuous troubling
>> Of his imagery.
> ......

Mildness, amid the neo-Neitzschean clatter,
His sense of graduations,
Quite out of place amid
Resistance to current exacerbations

Invitation, mere invitation to perceptivity
Gradually led him to the isolation
Which these presents place
Under a more tolerant, perhaps,
examination.

By constant elimination
The manifest universe
Yielded an armour
Against utter consternation,

A Minoan undulation,
Seen, we admit, amid ambrosial
circumstances

Strengthened him against
The discouraging doctrine of chances

And his desire for survival,
Faint in the most strenuous moods,
Became an Olympian *apathein*
In the presence of selected perceptions.

A pale gold, in the aforesaid pattern,
The unexpected palms
Destroying, certainly, the artist's urge,
Left him delighted with the imaginary
Audition of the phantasmal sea-surge,

Incapable of the least utterance or composition,
Emendation, conservation of the "better tradition",
Refinement of medium, elimination of superfluities,
August attraction or concentration.

Nothing in brief, but maudlin confession
Irresponse to human aggression,
Amid the precipitation, down-float
Of insubstantial manna

Lifting the faint susurrus
Of his subjective hosannah.

Ultimate affronts to human redundancies;

Non-esteem of self-styled "his betters"
Leading, as he well knew,
To his final
Exclusion from the world of letters.

IV.

SCATTERED Moluccas
Not knowing, day to day,
The first day's end, in the next noon;
The placid water
Unbroken by the Simoon;

Thick foliage
Placid beneath warm suns,
Tawn fore-shores
Washed in the cobalt of oblivions;

Or through dawn-mist
The grey and rose
Of the juridical
Flamingoes;

A consciousness disjunct,
Being but this overblotted
Series
Of intermittences;

Coracle of Pacific voyages,
The unforecasted beach:
Then on an oar
Read this:

"I was
And I no more exist;
Here drifted
An hedonist."

MEDALLION

LUINI in porcelain!
The grand piano
Utters a profane
Protest with her clear soprano.

The sleek head emerges
From the gold-yellow frock
As Anadyomene in the opening
Pages of Reinach.

Honey-red, closing the face-oval
A basket-work of braids which seem as if they were
Spun in King Minos' hall
From metal, or intractable amber;

The face-oval beneath the glaze,
Bright in its suave bounding-line, as
Beneath half-watt rays
The eyes turn topaz.

CPSIA information can be obtained
at www.ICGtesting.com
Printed in the USA
LVHW081557080221
678723LV00011B/624